"Hey, kid," Jake growled at T.J., "we got in trouble because of you today. You shouldn't have told Coach Bob that we put your shoes up on the high dive. This time, it's not gonna be your shoes. It's gonna be your head!"

"That's right, T.J!" cried Matt Rogers. "We're gonna get you!"

The two big boys advanced toward T.J. Sinister grins covered their faces. T.J. backed away. He frantically looked around for help, but there were only younger children around him.

Finally, T.J. backed himself up against a wall of the pool. He could go no further. Jake and Matt closed in on him.

"Help!" T.J. blurted an instant before outstretched arms seized him around the neck.

TROUBLE
IN THE DEEP END

NANCY SIMPSON LEVENE

Chariot Books™ is an imprint of Chariot Family Publishing
Cook Communications Ministries, Elgin, Illinois 60120
Cook Communications Ministries, Paris, Ontario
Kingsway Communications, Eastbourne, England

TROUBLE IN THE DEEP END

Designed by Elizabeth Thompson
First Printing, 1993
Printed in the United States of America
97 96 95 94 5 4 3

Library of Congress Cataloging-in-Publication Data
Levene, Nancy S. 1949-
Trouble in the deep end / by Nancy Simpson Levene.
p. cm.
Summary: While at the swimming pool, T.J. and Zack try to deal with the annoying attacks of some older bullies on the swim team.
ISBN 0-7814-0701-X
[1. Bullies—Fiction. 2. Swimming—Fiction. 3. Christian life—Fiction.] I. Title.
PZ7.L5724Tad 1993
[Fic]—dc20 93-16602
CIP
AC

To Jesus,
who holds my heart in His hands
and makes it like His own
and
To my mother, Jane Simpson,
who cared for me from the beginning
and whose love I shall always cherish.

Listen, all of you. Love your enemies. Do good to those who hate you. Pray for the happiness of those who curse you; implore God's blessing on those who hurt you.

Luke 6:27, 28

ACKNOWLEDGMENTS

Thank you, Cara, for contributing so much to this series. I am thankful to have a daughter whose heart is much like Jesus'. With love from your mother.

CONTENTS

1

TROUBLE ON THE HIGH DIVE

"Hey, cut it out! Give me back my towel!" T.J.'s best friend, Zack, struggled desperately against a group of older boys. Zack tried to hold on to his beach towel while the older boys slowly wrenched it away from him.

T.J. ran to help his friend but got there too late. Zack lost his grip on the towel. The older boys laughed loudly as they wadded it into a ball and threw it into the swimming pool.

"Too bad, kid," one of the older boys laughed. "That's what you get for bringing a Batman towel to swim practice."

"Yeah, you better go save Batman!" hollered another.

"You jerks!" T.J. yelled at them. The older boys glared at T.J., but he didn't care. The group of twelve-year-old boys had been a real problem for the swim team this year. The oldest swimmers

didn't pay any attention to them, so they seemed to think they ran things. They bullied and shoved their way around, making life miserable for the younger team members. No one liked them, and everyone was getting tired of it, including the head of the swim team, Coach Bob.

"I saw that! I saw that!" Coach Bob suddenly ran down a set of steps that separated the pool from the lounge and snack bar area. He blew the whistle that hung around his neck. Everyone froze on the spot.

"I want you boys in the water!" Coach Bob snapped at the group of twelve year olds. When they didn't move immediately, the coach yelled, "NOW!"

The boys jumped into the water.

"Go get that towel," Coach Bob demanded.

The older boys hurried to fish Zack's beach towel out of the water. They handed it to the coach. Coach Bob wrung the water out of the towel and hung it on a lawn chair to dry.

"You will swim ten laps, the length of the pool," he told the twelve-year-old boys. "The rest of us will enjoy watching you." The coach and the other swimmers sat down at the side of the pool.

"On your mark. Get set. Go!" Coach Bob blew his whistle. The twelve-year-old boys began to swim.

T.J. and Zack laughed and laughed as they watched the older boys splash through the water. As the pool was Olympic size, it would be a good workout.

After their ten-lap swim, the twelve-year-old boys seemed too tired to give anyone further trouble. T.J. and Zack joined the younger swimmers in the shallow end of the pool while the older ones worked out in the deep end.

That morning, Coach Bob let his four-year-old son, Derek, work out with the team. T.J. watched

Derek in amazement. He looked so little in the water, but he swam the freestyle back and forth the width of the pool.

"I'm going to have Derek race in the five and under group at the next swim meet," Coach Bob told the team proudly.

"It's a good thing you turned six last spring," T.J. teased his younger brother, Charley. "Otherwise, you'd have to race against Derek!"

"Aw," Charley wrinkled his nose. There was no way he would let a four year old beat him.

When Coach Bob called an end to practice, T.J. and Charley ran to grab their towels and shoes. They were supposed to meet Mother and their little sisters in the snack bar area for an early lunch.

T.J. quickly found his towel, but he could not find his tennis shoes. He was sure he had left them sitting beside his towel, but now they were not there.

"Where could they be?" T.J. demanded in a loud voice.

"Beats me," Charley shrugged.

"Maybe you kicked 'em off somewhere else," Zack suggested.

"No, I remember I put them right here by my towel," T.J. insisted.

"Well, your shoes can't have just disappeared," replied Zack, sounding a little too much like a grown-up for T.J.

"They're not here, are they?" T.J. spread his arms open wide to show Zack that he had no other answer.

A sudden burst of laughter caught the boys' attention. Looking behind him, T.J. saw the same group of twelve-year-old boys who had given him and Zack so much trouble at practice.

"What's the matter, T.J.?" one of the older boys jeered. "Lose something?"

"You better look around, nerd-brain," another told him.

"Yeah, look up high in the air!" cried a third.

"HA! HA! HA!" the group of twelve year olds laughed. They ran off across the pool area.

T.J., Zack, and Charley watched them go. T.J. was puzzled.

"What did they mean, 'look up high in the air'?" he asked Zack.

"Aw, who knows what those creeps ever mean," replied Zack disgustedly.

"It sounds like they took my shoes and put them somewhere weird," T.J. worried.

"It sure does," agreed Zack.

"I see them!" Charley cried out excitedly.

While T.J. and Zack had been talking, Charley had been looking for the shoes. "Look up there!" Charley pointed across the way to the diving pool.

T.J. squinted. He could just barely see the tops of his tennis shoes where they were perched at the very edge of the high diving board.

"I can't believe it!" T.J. groaned. "Why would they put my shoes up there?"

"Because they are complete nerds," was Zack's answer. "I guess you'll have to go get them."

T.J. sighed and ran over to the diving pool. He hurriedly climbed the steep, tall steps of the high dive and stepped onto the board itself. Although T.J. had jumped off the same board several times in the past, it was a little different trying to rescue something off the end of it.

The board jiggled and bounced with every step. The closer he got to the shoes, the more the board bounced. To keep his shoes from falling off and plunging into the water below, T.J. finally had to crawl on his hands and knees to the end of the board.

It was a long, slow crawl. The board wobbled and bounced. T.J. felt like he was caught high on a mountain bridge with nothing but a thin narrow board separating him from the roaring waters below. To make matters worse, Zack and Charley began to laugh uproariously at T.J.'s predicament. Soon, T.J. was fighting the urge to giggle himself. It only made the board shake more.

"Hey, T.J.!" Zack suddenly appeared behind T.J. at the top of the diving board's steps. "I'm here to help you!"

"NO!" T.J. frantically tried to wave his friend away. "Get off the board! You're making it bounce too much!"

"But, T.J., this looks like fun!" Zack laughed. He got down on his hands and knees and began to move toward T.J. at the end of the board.

"NO! Go back! Go back!" T.J. cried. The board shook so much he had to grab hold tightly to the end of it to keep from falling off. One of T.J.'s shoes bounced off the board and splashed into the water below.

"Zack, you dummy!" T.J. gasped. "See what you did?"

He and his friend balanced together on hands and knees at the end of the high diving board. Soon, they could not keep from laughing. They laughed and laughed, and the board shook dangerously with every giggle.

T.J. was so weak from laughing that all he

could do was hang on to the board. Suddenly, Charley showed up and added his weight to the board as he stepped out on it. But before T.J. could say anything to his brother, the piercing shriek of a whistle sounded from below.

"WHAT DO YOU THINK YOU'RE DOING UP THERE?" hollered a familiar voice.

"Uh oh, we've had it," warned Zack.

T.J. sighed. He was afraid Zack was right. That voice belonged to none other than Coach Bob. T.J. was sure his swim coach would not approve of three boys on the high dive at once, especially when the swimming pool had not officially opened for the day and there were no lifeguards on duty.

"T.J., ZACK, AND CHARLEY, GET DOWN FROM THERE IMMEDIATELY!" cried T.J.'s mother.

"Oh, no," groaned T.J. He glanced at his mother. She stood right beside Coach Bob, with her hands on her hips and a frown on her face. Neither his coach nor his mother looked very happy.

"COMING!" Charley suddenly yelled to Mother. He turned and hopped back along the high diving board to the steps.

"CHARLEY! STOP JIGGLING THE BOARD!" T.J. cried.

"CUT IT OUT, CHARLEY!" Zack hollered.

But it was too late. The board jerked violently. The two boys lost their balance and toppled off the board, falling headfirst into the water below!

2

ATTACK BY BULLIES

"T.J.! What were you boys doing on the high diving board?" Mother asked as she and Coach Bob helped T.J. and Zack out of the water.

"I was trying to get my shoes," T.J. spluttered. He had hit the water hard and flat. There was a big, red spot on his stomach and chest.

"Your shoes?" Mother looked puzzled. "What do your shoes have to do with the high diving board?"

"Nothing, usually," T.J. made a sour face, "except when somebody steals your shoes and puts them up there."

"What?" Mother exclaimed. "Who would do that?"

"Those creeps from the swim team," put in Zack before T.J. could reply.

"What creeps from the swim team?" Coach Bob asked.

"Oh, you know, Jake Flaherty, Matt Rogers, Tim Evans . . ." Zack began naming off a list of the twelve-year-old boys.

"I believe I had better have another talk with those boys," Coach Bob frowned.

"Where are your shoes now?" Mother asked T.J.

T.J. shrugged and pointed at the water. "They gotta be at the bottom of the pool."

"Great!" Mother replied. "Can you get them?"

"Oh, sure," both boys told her. They jumped back into the diving pool and, with Coach Bob's help, rescued the shoes.

Mother poured the water out of the shoes. They said good-bye to Coach Bob, and Zack went home. Mother, T.J., Charley, and their sisters went to the snack bar area for lunch.

T.J. ate his hamburger quickly. After the swim team workout and the excitement of the high dive, he was hungry. So was Charley. Mother had to buy them an extra hamburger and french fries to share. T.J. also drank down a large milk shake.

"Goodness!" Mother commented as soon as the boys finished eating. "You must have been hungry. There isn't a crumb left! I think after that big lunch, you had better not go back in the water for a while."

"Oh, Mom," Charley complained.

"Why don't you join your sisters in the smaller pools?" Mother suggested.

"In the baby pools?" T.J. and Charley gasped. "Are you kidding?"

"You don't have to go in the smallest pool," Mother smiled at them. "You can take Elizabeth and Megan into the middle-sized pool. It would be just for a little while. That way, I can relax in the sun."

Mother smiled and waved good-bye as T.J. and Charley led Megan and Elizabeth down the steps to the pool area.

There might be one good thing about this, T.J. thought. *Mothers never forget when you do them a favor, and they will usually reward you for it.*

The middle-sized pool was only for children ages five and under, but T.J. and Charley could swim in it because they were taking care of their sisters. The pool started shallow, but its water rose to three feet at the deeper end.

T.J. and Charley took their sisters to the deepest part to play. Elizabeth could not touch the bottom, so T.J. put her on his back. Soon he was playing the part of a bucking bronco, a whale, and then a motorboat. With Elizabeth on his back, he chased Megan and Charley around the pool. Then Megan wanted a turn. T.J. played the game until he was exhausted. He sent Charley to get one of Elizabeth's inner tubes and Megan's beach ball.

The boys and Megan played catch with the beach ball while Elizabeth floated around in her tube. T.J. was surprised at how well Megan dove for the ball and how she was able to catch it. His four-year-old sister seemed fearless. She dove here and there, often slipping under the water, and not caring if she came up with a mouthful of water. When they played a game of tag, she surprised him even more. Megan was hard to catch. Her speed in the water was almost equal to Charley's.

As T.J. watched Megan, he suddenly had an idea. It might be goofy. It might not work, but it was worth a try.

"Megan, come here a minute," T.J. called to his sister.

Megan hopped across the pool on her tiptoes. When she reached T.J., she smacked him in the face with a water-soaked foam ball. She and Charley laughed as T.J. wiped the water from his eyes.

"Come on, cut it out, Megan," T.J. growled. "I want to see if you can do something."

"Do what?" Megan frowned.

"I want to see if you can swim," T.J. replied.

"Sure I can swim," Megan told him, "but I want to play ball."

"Megan, this is important," T.J. insisted. "Show me how you can swim. Can you swim from this side of the pool to the other side?"

"Oh, sure, that's easy," Megan answered, warming up to the idea. It wasn't often that her big brother wanted to watch her do something. Taking a big gulp of air, Megan swam across the pool.

"That was good, Megan," T.J. moved to his sister's side. "Now watch me as I swim across the pool. Watch and see how I move my arms and kick my feet."

T.J. swam the freestyle across the pool. When he reached the other side, he said to Megan, "Now you try and swim just like I did."

"Okay," Megan agreed. Once again, she made her way across the pool.

"That was much better," T.J. praised his sister. "This time, try and turn your head to the side to take a breath. See, like this." T.J. demonstrated the correct way to breathe. He had Megan practice it while standing up in the pool.

"T.J., what are you doing? Are you giving

Megan a swimming lesson?" Charley interrupted.

"Look, Charley," T.J. said in a low voice, "I think with some good coaching, Megan could be an awesome swimmer. I think she could even be as good as Coach Bob's son Derek. When she gets good enough, I'm gonna ask Mom and Dad to enter her in a swim meet!"

T.J. turned to his younger sister. "What do you think, Megan? Would you like to swim in a real race?"

"Yeah!" Megan cried, clapping her hands together happily.

"You mean enter her in the five and unders at a real swim meet?" Charley asked amazed. "But Megan's only four years old!"

"No problem," T.J. replied confidently. "Derek is only four years old and he's going to swim in the five and unders at the next swim meet. Coach Bob said so himself."

"I know, but Megan's never even had swimming lessons," Charley objected.

"So what?" T.J. retorted. "I can teach her."

"Oh, boy," Charley sighed. "This I gotta see."

T.J. ignored his brother. Charley could be such a pain sometimes. He always had to have scientific proof for everything!

Megan listened to T.J. and tried to do

everything he told her to do. After several trips across the pool, Megan's strokes and breathing had improved so much that even Charley had to agree with T.J. Megan was a natural!

T.J. was concentrating so hard on Megan's swimming progress that he forgot the time. He even forgot that he was in the children's pool.

Suddenly, a voice startled him. "Gee, T.J., it's awfully sweet of you to give swimming lessons," it hissed.

"Do you enjoy playing in the baby pool, T.J.?" asked a second voice.

T.J. whirled around. He stared up into the faces of Jake Flaherty and Matt Rogers, leaders of the group of twelve-year-old boys who had caused T.J. and Zack so much trouble that morning.

"Hey, kid," Jake growled at T.J., "we got in trouble because of you today. You shouldn't have told Coach Bob that we put your shoes up on the high dive. This time, it's not gonna be your shoes. It's gonna be your head!"

"That's right, T.J!" cried Matt Rogers. "We're gonna get you!"

The two big boys advanced toward T.J. Sinister grins covered their faces. T.J. backed away. He frantically looked around for help, but there were only younger children nearby.

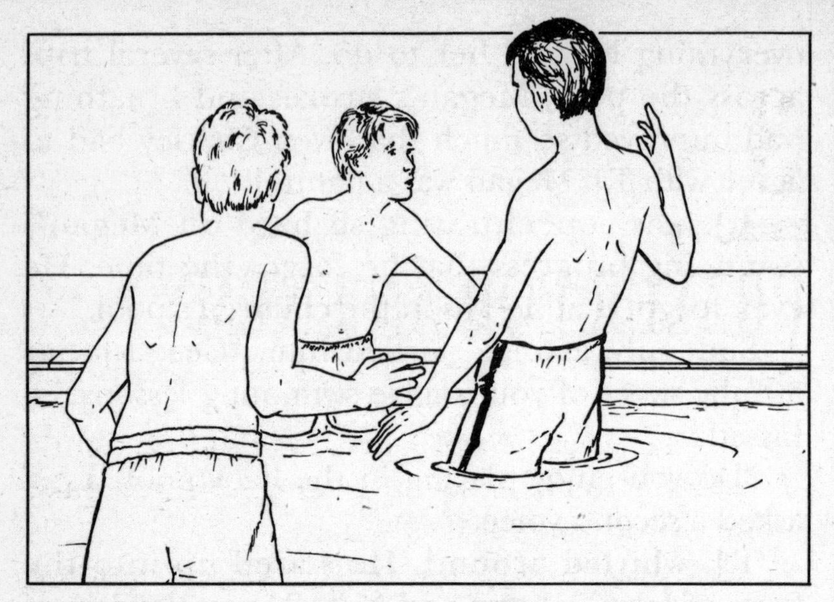

Finally, T.J. backed himself up against a wall of the pool. He could go no further. Jake and Matt closed in on him.

"Help!" T.J. blurted an instant before outstretched arms seized him around the neck.

3

PRAYER FOR AN ENEMY

T.J. winced as he felt Jake's hands close tightly around his neck. A second later, however, Jake suddenly released his hold on T.J.

"Hey! Cut it out!" the bully hollered, holding his hands up to shield his eyes from a stream of water that hit him full in the face.

T.J. turned his head to see who had come to his rescue. He was surprised to see his little sister Megan holding a water pistol. She was busy pumping a steady flow of water into Jake's face!

The next moment, Charley threw Elizabeth's Daisy Duck inner tube around Jake's neck and jerked the bully violently backward off his feet. Charley wrapped his arms and legs around Jake's neck and would not let go.

Matt tried to pull Charley off of Jake, but T.J., recovering his wits, dove at Matt. With both fists flailing, T.J. drove the second bully away

from his brother and sisters.

"SHHHREEEEK!" a lifeguard blew a loud whistle. She stormed into the water but had to call a second lifeguard to help restore order to the swimming pool.

A crowd of spectators watched as the lifeguards separated the boys and tried to find out what had happened.

"T.J! Charley!" Mother called, hurrying over to her children. "What is going on?" Mother lifted Elizabeth into her arms as the little girl began to cry.

"They're always picking on kids!" T.J. told the

lifeguards, pointing his finger at Jake and Matt. "They are nothing but bullies. You can ask Coach Bob about them."

T.J. then turned to his mother. "They're the ones who threw Zack's towel in the water and put my shoes up on the high dive. They got mad because I told Coach Bob about them. They came in here and tried to hurt me and Charley."

"I'm sure he's right," Mother said to the lifeguards. "Coach Bob has had trouble with some of the older boys on the swimming team. Some of them did put my son's shoes up on the high dive today. The coach had to help T.J. rescue his shoes out of the diving pool."

"We will talk to the coach about this," said one of the lifeguards. "Come on, you two," she motioned for Jake and Matt to follow her.

"But what about them?" Jake pointed angrily at T.J. and Charley. "They were fighting too! They tried to hurt us."

The lifeguard stared at the two older boys. "Give me a break," was all she said in reply. She and the other lifeguard led the two bullies away.

When T.J. and Charley got home from the pool that afternoon, they ran next door to Zack's house to tell him all about the fight with Jake and

Matt. The boys stayed at Zack's house quite late, discussing their troubles with the older boys and wondering what Coach Bob would do about it. Finally, Zack's mother called Zack to dinner. T.J. and Charley hurried to their own house.

"Well, you made it home after all," Mother called to the boys from the kitchen. "I was just about ready to send the Sergeant out after you!"

T.J. and Charley grinned. Sergeant was the name of their big German shepherd. He used to be a real army dog. Mother called him 'the Sergeant' whenever she wanted the dog to perfom an official duty for her like fetching the newspaper or bringing home children who were late for dinner.

T.J. ran into the kitchen, slid across the floor, and tackled the big dog. Sergeant was only slightly disturbed. He gave T.J. a quick lick but then returned to his present duty. He was hungrily helping Mother count the pieces of chicken as she spooned them out of a pan and onto a platter.

"You can't do anything with Sergeant when there's food around," T.J. sighed.

"Why don't you feed him?" Mother suggested. "He might just take his eyes off the chicken for a few seconds and I could finish up dinner without having to step around the dog all the time."

"Okay," T.J. agreed. He grabbed Sergeant's food bowl and went to the garage for the dog food. For once, Sergeant did not follow him but stayed in the kitchen with the chicken. When T.J. returned to the kitchen with the bowl of dog food, the big dog ate hurriedly, keeping one eye on the chicken at all times.

Father came downstairs for dinner, having changed his clothes after work. The family sat down in the dining room, Sergeant taking his usual place beside T.J.'s chair. Everyone joined hands and thanked God for their food. Then, even before the food was put on their plates, T.J. and Charley began telling Father all about the fight at the swimming pool.

"You should have seen it, Dad!" T.J. cried excitedly. "Megan hit Jake full force right in the face with water from the water pistol, and Charley wrapped Elizabeth's inner tube around his neck. Jake looked real cute with Daisy Duck on his head. Ha! Ha! It was awesome!"

"Yeah," Charley agreed. "I hung onto Jake and wouldn't let go. But you should've seen T.J. He fought off Matt with just his fists. I've never seen anybody move that fast, even in the movies!"

"I was mad," T.J. admitted. "At first I was scared when they both came at me in the pool. But then I got mad and decided they weren't going to hurt us anymore."

"I can understand how you felt," Father nodded. "There are times when you may need to defend yourself or others around you. But always make sure that you are on the defensive and not the offensive side. Never start a fight. Try to avoid a fight at all costs. Remember, we are Christians, and Jesus said we are to love our enemies and to pray for them."

"How can I love someone like Jake Flaherty?" T.J. wanted to know.

"That seems like a hard thing to do," Father admitted. "I think we can only love people like that with the special love God gives us through Jesus, His Son. We need to use Jesus' love, not our own, to love our enemies. Tonight, let's ask God if He will give you the love of Jesus. Then you can try saying a prayer for Jake."

T.J. wrinkled his nose. "Well, okay. I'll try it."

That night, T.J. and Charley played their usual summer evening game of hide-and-seek with the neighborhood children. They each took a quick bath and then climbed the two flights of stairs to T.J.'s loft bedroom on the third floor of the house. T.J. had the only bedroom on the third floor. It was a long, rectangular room, and the ceiling slanted on one side down to a double set of windows.

During the summer, Charley usually slept in T.J.'s bedroom instead of his own. The boys enjoyed many nights whispering in their new bunks, staying awake as long as they could manage.

"Tonight it's my turn to sleep in the top bunk," Charley informed T.J.

T.J. shrugged. He pretended not to care even though everyone knows the top bunk is the best. The boys exchanged pillows. T.J. sighed and bounced onto the lower bunk.

Father and Mother usually took turns listening to the boys' prayers. Tonight it was Father's turn. He came in and sat on the bottom bunk with T.J.

Charley said his prayers first. T.J. said his usual prayers, and then Father prayed, "Dear Father in heaven, please give us the love of Jesus so that we can love and pray for our enemies as Jesus told us to do. We pray in the name of Jesus. Amen."

T.J. looked up at Father. "Do you think we got it? Do you think God gave us the love of Jesus?"

Father smiled. "I'm sure He did. Why don't

you say a prayer for Jake? It sounds like he needs God in his life."

"I don't know what to say," T.J. frowned.

"Maybe you could ask God to help you out with Jake," suggested Father. "Ask Him to help Jake not be such a bully."

"Okay," T.J. agreed. "Dear Lord Jesus," he prayed, "please help Jake not to be a bully anymore. Help him not to fight or pick on kids anymore, especially not on me. I pray in Your name. Amen."

"Very good," said Father. "I don't see how the Lord could refuse to answer that prayer."

After Father had left, T.J. yawned and stretched. *I sure hope the Lord does something about Jake,* he thought right before falling asleep. *I don't know if I can take this much longer.*

The next morning it looked as if the Lord had answered T.J.'s prayer. Jake and Matt were not at swim practice. In fact, the two bullies did not come to practice for the rest of the week. The other twelve-year-old boys glared at T.J., but they did not say or do anything to him.

Just when T.J. began to hope that he would never see their faces again, Jake and Matt returned to swim practice the following week.

Most of the other team members were not pleased to see them either.

"I thought we got rid of those jerks," T.J. heard some of the older girls complain.

"Looks like we're in for it again," Zack sighed. T.J. and Charley scowled.

For a while, however, the older boys behaved themselves. It seemed that they had been given a stern warning by Coach Bob. T.J. tried to ignore them and stay out of their way, so things went along fairly well.

Without having to worry so much about Jake and his friends, T.J. began to concentrate on teaching Megan her swimming strokes. He and Charley worked with her every day. Finally, the boys thought she was ready to swim for Coach Bob. They asked the coach if he would watch Megan and decide if she were good enough to join the swimming team.

"Can you have her here right after practice tomorrow?" Coach Bob asked the boys.

"Okay, that would be great," T.J. replied. That would give him the rest of the day to fine-tune Megan's strokes.

T.J. and Charley were worse than two mother hens that afternoon. They coached Megan so much that even she grew tired.

"I just can't seem to teach her how to do a proper racing dive," T.J. complained to Mother that evening. "She either dives too deep or does a belly flop."

"I wouldn't worry about it too much," Mother replied. "Megan will learn how to dive soon enough. After all, she's only four years old."

The next morning, T.J. and Charley waited anxiously for practice to end. As they watched four-year-old Derek work out with the team, they were sure Megan could do just as well. If only their coach would agree.

Megan and Mother were at the pool's side the moment practice was over. Megan looked ready to swim. She even wore an old pair of T.J.'s goggles.

"I hear you have an Olympic champion in the making," Coach Bob said to Mother as he pointed at Megan.

Mother laughed. "The boys think so. They're ready to enter her into competition."

"Very good," said Coach Bob. He knelt down in front of Megan. "How old are you?"

"Four," Megan answered rather shyly.

"Would you like to show me how you can swim?" Coach Bob asked her.

"Okay," replied Megan.

T.J. led Megan over to the side of the pool. They were both nervous. To make matters worse, several of the swim team members were still hanging around the pool, including Jake and the group of twelve-year-old boys.

"Don't be scared," T.J. told his younger sister, trying to keep her calm in spite of his nervousness. "Dive in and swim across the pool just like we practiced."

Megan nodded. She adjusted her goggles as she had seen the older children do. Then she stepped up to the pool's edge, took a deep breath, and belly flopped into the water.

"Isn't she cute?" several girls cried at once.

T.J. frowned. Megan just couldn't get that dive right. She was swimming well, however. T.J. felt an older brother's pride as he watched his sister fly across the water. Megan was so light and quick that it looked like she was swimming on top of the water and not in it.

Megan reached the other side of the pool in no time. Everyone clapped and cheered for her. Looking at Coach Bob, T.J. could tell that his coach was impressed.

"Very good," Coach Bob called to Megan. "Can you swim back to this side now?"

Megan nodded and pushed off from the side of the pool just as T.J. had taught her. She quickly swam back to the other side.

"Excellent!" Coach Bob exclaimed. "Watch out, you guys," he told the older swimmers. "This little girl may pass you all up!"

The other swimmers laughed.

"Why don't you bring Megan to swim practice with you every day?" Coach Bob suggested to T.J. "She can work out with Derek."

"All right!" T.J. replied. He and Charley smacked their hands together in a sign of victory. They had done it! They had coached Megan well.

Mother laughed. "I didn't think I would have three children on the team so soon," she told Coach Bob. "But if you think Megan is good enough, that's fine with me."

"I am sure she is good enough," replied Coach Bob. "My only worry is that she might beat Derek!"

Everyone laughed. They got Megan out of the pool and got ready to go home. Mother and the girls walked on ahead. T.J. and Charley followed, carrying their towels and shoes. As T.J. walked past the group of twelve-year-old boys, rude comments filled his ears.

"Hey, T.J., how many more kids you got in your

nursery school?" one of the older boys teased.

"Isn't that cute?" cried another boy. "It's Daddy T.J. and his little girl!"

"Hey, T.J., you wanna teach me how to swim?" called out another.

T.J. felt his ears grow hot as he listened to the taunts. Those boys could spoil anything. He had felt so happy just a moment before, but now he felt like punching somebody. When would they leave him alone?

4

SMASHED GOGGLES

At Monday's practice, Coach Bob announced that the first swim meet of the season would be held Friday night at their own pool, Kingswood Country Club. It was to be a small meet. Only one other swimming team would be participating.

The boys were excited. They were always ready to race against competitors and were glad that the season was officially beginning. T.J., Zack, and Charley worked hard to increase their swimming speed. So did Megan. T.J. tried his best to smooth out Megan's racing dive.

Finally, the big night arrived. T.J., Charley, and Megan got to the pool early to do warm-up laps and stretching exercises with Coach Bob and the rest of the team. The races started promptly at seven o'clock with the youngest swimmers swimming first. That meant that Megan was in the first race of the evening.

"Now don't worry," T.J. told his small sister. "Just dive in and swim across the pool like at practice."

"Okay, okay," Megan replied confidently. She did not seem a bit concerned, and that worried T.J.

"Megan, are you sure you know what to do?" T.J. asked one more time.

"Sure, no problem," replied Megan.

"Okay, now look, you gotta watch where you're going or you'll get tangled in the ropes," T.J. instructed, although he had said that very same thing many times before.

"I know, I know," Megan twirled a pair of goggles in her hand.

"And don't raise your head up to breathe. Just turn it to the side," T.J. added.

"I know," Megan sighed.

"One more thing," added T.J., "keep your head down between your arms when you dive. Don't look up or you'll belly flop."

"I know! You've already told me that a million times!" Megan frowned and stomped her way over to the pool.

T.J. watched her go. He sighed. Maybe he didn't want to be a swimming coach when he grew up after all. T.J. positioned himself across the pool from Megan. As the younger children only swam a single lap, he would be there when Megan finished.

The five-and-under age-group did not use the big starting blocks. At the start of the race, they could jump in the water, dive, or push off from the side. T.J. noticed that only one other swimmer besides Megan and Derek was positioned to begin the race with a dive.

Suddenly the starting gun fired! The race began!

"Please, God, please, God . . ." was all T.J. could say as he watched his little sister make the best dive of her life and come up swimming for all she was worth.

T.J. found his voice and shouted for joy as Megan quickly flew ahead of everyone in the race. There was no stopping her as she swam a straight line to the other side of the pool, finishing a good body length ahead of the other swimmers, including Derek, Coach Bob's son. On top of it all, she had not taken a single breath the entire distance!

"Megan!" T.J. shouted and leaped into the water beside her. "You won! Did you forget to breathe?"

"Yes," she nodded and gasped for breath.

Everyone around them began to laugh.

"That was a wonderful race, Megan," Coach Bob told her. "Congratulations, T.J.! You did a fine job of coaching. If I ever need an assistant, I know who to ask."

T.J. beamed with pleasure. He took Megan back to where the rest of the family was sitting. Mother and Father praised them both.

Next came Charley's first race. T.J. cheered loudly for his brother. Even though the butterfly stroke was not one of Charley's best, he still managed to come in second out of six swimmers.

The butterfly, however, was T.J.'s best stroke, and he eagerly waited for his first race to begin. Last year, he had won all of his butterfly races, and he was determined to do the same this summer.

Just as his race was called, T.J. threw off his towel and reached for his goggles. He thought he had left them beside his shoes but they were not there. Searching frantically, T.J. looked all around the chairs and in the family swimming bag.

"I guess you'll have to swim without them," said Mother as the final call for T.J.'s race was announced and T.J. had still not found the goggles.

"But I can't swim without them!" T.J. wailed.

"Coach Bob wants us always to wear goggles. He says if we don't, the chlorine gets in our eyes and we can't see to swim a straight line."

"Well, this time you'll have to swim without them or not swim at all," Father told him.

"I could borrow Charley's," T.J. thought out loud. He looked around for his brother, but Charley had run off with some of his friends. His goggles were nowhere in sight.

"How about borrowing Megan's?" Mother suggested.

"I can't wear those goggles," T.J. replied. "They're too little. They give me a headache."

"T.J. Fairbanks, please report to the starting blocks," a sudden voice called over the loud speaker.

"Oh, great!" T.J. cried. He ran to the starting blocks and climbed up on the one assigned to his lane. He felt completely unprepared for the race. He had not had time to get in the water before the race to get his body used to the water temperature. He was flustered and upset over losing his goggles. He looked around. He was the only one on the starting blocks without them.

Glancing to the side, T.J. saw Coach Bob looking at him oddly. Positioning himself for the dive, T.J. looked directly across the pool and

noticed a group of faces grinning at him in a most unpleasant way. It was Jake and his friends. T.J. wondered if they had anything to do with his missing goggles. He stared at the group of boys so intently that he forgot to pay attention to the countdown before the race. The loud bang of the starting gun caught T.J. off guard. As the other swimmers dove swiftly into the water, T.J. lost his balance and belly flopped!

Even in the cool water, T.J. felt his face burn with embarrassment. He'd never live down that belly flop. Everyone would have seen it—the coach, the mean boys, the other swimmers on his team—everyone! T.J. wished he could stay in the water forever and never come out again. He tried to make up for the bad dive by swimming his hardest, but without his goggles, he could not see and ran into the ropes that marked off his swimming lane. All in all, the race was a total disaster. T.J., the favored swimmer, the one most likely to win the race, came in dead last.

Keeping his head down, T.J. crawled out of the pool and made his way to the other side, avoiding everyone he knew. He refused to look at anyone. Hurrying down a flight of steps at the rear of the diving pool, T.J. entered the boys' locker room. He rushed into one of the bathroom stalls.

Although he tried to keep them back, the tears began to fall from his eyes. It was not fair! He had worked hard to get ready for the race. It should have been his best race, but it had ended up the worst. And all because something had happened to his goggles. Had he lost them, or had Jake and his buddies taken them?

All was quiet in the boys' locker room as T.J. thought over and over about his missing goggles and losing his race. T.J. thought he was alone until, quite suddenly, an object was hurled over the door of the bathroom stall. It just missed hitting the toilet and landed KERPLUNK! at T.J.'s feet. T.J. recognized the object at once. It was his goggles!

Picking them up, T.J. stared at them in disbelief. They had been smashed and shattered beyond repair. It looked as if someone had taken a hammer to them. Someone had deliberately destroyed his goggles and caused him to lose the race!

The longer T.J. stared at his broken goggles, the angrier he became. He burst out of the bathroom stall, loudly banging the door open. Marching through the locker room and up the stairs, T.J. clenched his fists tightly. He knew who had done this to him, and that person was going to pay for it. He didn't care how big or how mean Jake Flaherty was. He was still going to pay for this!

Just as T.J. reached the top step, a large hand gripped his arm. Not caring who it was and almost wishing it was Jake, T.J. lunged at the figure before him, his fists and feet flying.

"Ow! Take it easy! T.J., stop it!" cried a familiar voice. Strong arms pinned T.J.'s arms to his sides and lifted him completely off of his feet. Startled, T.J. looked up into the puzzled face of his father.

"What is the matter with you?" Father exclaimed. "Your mother sent me here to look for you. We thought you might be upset about the race, but I didn't think you would attack me!"

"I didn't know it was you," T.J. mumbled, turning his head to avoid his father's gaze. At that moment, all the disappointment, hurt, and anger crashed down on T.J. A giant sob escaped from his lips, and before he could stop them, rivers of tears flowed from his eyes.

Father carried T.J. down the stairs and back into the boys' locker room. He closed the door behind them so they would not be disturbed. Sitting down on a bench, Father held T.J. close until the tears stopped.

"Do you want to tell me what happened?" Father asked.

T.J. held out his hand for Father to see. In it was the pair of smashed and broken goggles.

"How did your goggles get broken?" Father asked.

T.J. shrugged. "I dunno," he said. His voice sounded dry and raspy. "Somebody took them and broke them on purpose! I think it was Jake." T.J. then told his father about seeing Jake and his friends from the starting block and how they had grinned at him. He told how he had been so upset about his dive and the missing goggles that he couldn't swim and lost the race. He told his father how someone had thrown the mangled pair of goggles into the bathroom stall where T.J. had stood alone.

"I would say that this whole matter with Jake has gone too far," Father frowned after hearing T.J.'s story. "Right after the swim meet, you and I are going to have a talk with Coach Bob. We will show him your goggles and tell him everything you have told me."

"I want to tell him now and make him kick Jake out of the swim meet!" T.J. declared.

"No, we can't do that," Father patted T.J.'s shoulder. "We don't know for sure that it was Jake who broke your goggles. We must act fairly."

"Why should I act fairly?" T.J. exploded. "Jake never acts fairly. He does all the mean, rotten things and gets away with them!"

"It may look like Jake is getting away with things, but he really isn't," Father replied. "The same Father in heaven who watches you as you try to live your life the right way also watches Jake. God sees all the bad things Jake does, and someday, Jake will have to answer for them. He will not get away with doing bad things forever."

"Well, I wish he wouldn't get away with smashing my goggles," T.J. said. "My butterfly race was ruined!"

"You will have lots of other butterfly races this summer," Father put an arm around T.J. He led him out the door of the locker room. "Come on, you have other races to swim tonight. It's probably just about time for your backstroke race."

"But what about my goggles?" T.J. asked his father.

"I'm sure Charley will be glad to share his goggles with you," smiled Father. He squeezed T.J.'s shoulder and then tickled his ribs.

T.J. laughed. His father always made things turn out right. T.J. was glad that he had a dad who was careful to do things the right way. It made T.J. feel safe and secure. That was worth more than winning all the swimming races put together.

"I'll race you up the stairs!" T.J. challenged his father and bounded up the steps two at a time.

"No fair, you got a head start!" Father cried. He chased T.J. up the stairs and they laughed and laughed when they reached the top at the same time.

5

A MUDDY SURPRISE

That weekend, T.J. tried to forget all about Jake and the broken goggles. The next day was Saturday. The family usually cooked dinner outside on the grill on Saturdays. Father was the main cook. That Saturday they were having Father's specialty—burgers and hot dogs.

T.J. invited Zack over for the cookout. Charley invited one of his friends in the neighborhood, a short sturdy little boy named Blake. All four of the boys and Sergeant were busy in the backyard playing a make-shift game of softball. Sergeant was the only outfielder. Although he was an excellent fielder, there was one drawback. Once Sergeant got the ball, he did not let go of it easily.

As soon as the grill was hot, Father carried out a big plate of hamburgers and began cooking. The boys immediately lost their outfielder. Sergeant was much more interested in the hamburgers than in the softball game. The big dog took up his station beside Father and the grill.

Megan and Elizabeth were also in the backyard. They were playing on the swingset and jungle gym. All of a sudden, Elizabeth fell off one of the swings, bumping her head on the ground.

"WAHHHHHH!" the little girl screamed at the top of her lungs. Father rushed over to the swingset and picked up Elizabeth. It took some time before she stopped crying and Father was able to calm her down. Walking back to the patio with Elizabeth in his arms, Father did not notice anything wrong until he turned to check the hamburgers on the grill.

"OH, NO!" T.J. and the boys heard Father shout. "THE HAMBURGERS ARE GONE!"

The boys rushed to the patio. They stared at the grill that had been full of hamburger patties. It was empty! Not a trace of hamburger could be seen.

Father and the boys stared at one another. They opened their mouths at the same time and cried one name, "SERGEANT!"

Searching the yard, it did not take them long to discover the hamburger thief. Behind a large bush in one corner of the yard sat the big German shepherd. He was hunched over, making terrible retching noises.

"Sergeant, what's the matter, boy?" T.J. and the others hurried up behind the dog. Sergeant cast a mournful eye at T.J.

"Leave him alone," Father told T.J. "He is sick to his stomach. It serves him right. That dog ate ten of my thick juicy hamburgers!"

"Maybe he learned a lesson," T.J. said hopefully as they returned to the patio with Father.

"I doubt it," was Father's reply.

That night, when the family ate their evening meal on the patio, things were rather unusual. Sergeant did not beg for handouts. He did not even look interested when Father returned again and again to the grill for more food. The dog lay in the yard at the edge of the patio and groaned. No one was too sympathetic, however. The dog's greediness had cost them a major part of their dinner. The family and their guests had to settle for hot dogs.

The following Monday, T.J. was back at swim practice. To his disappointment, so was Jake. T.J. had hoped that Jake would be kicked off the swimming team for stealing and ruining T.J.'s goggles. But Coach Bob had telephoned that weekend with other news. Jake had denied taking or breaking the goggles. There was no proof that he had committed the crime. The coach could do nothing about the broken goggles.

T.J. thought back to last Friday evening and the first swim meet of the summer. To his relief, no one had mentioned his belly flop, maybe because after losing so miserably in the butterfly race, T.J. had gone on to win first place in his freestyle and breaststroke races!

T.J. credited his father with the wins. Father's cheerful attitude had pulled T.J. out of the dumps and gave him strength to win the other races.

It's my family, T.J. thought. *It's my family who get me through the hard times.* He thought back to the time when he was attacked in the baby pool by Jake and Matt. His sister and brother had come through for him then—one with a water pistol and the other with an inner tube. T.J. grinned as he remembered how they had triumphed over Jake and Matt.

"Hey, what's so funny?" Zack asked T.J., jerking him out of his daydreams.

"Aw, nothing," T.J. told his best friend.

"Well, come on then. We gotta go swim laps."

"Okay, okay," T.J. followed Zack around to the side of the pool. Swimmers were busy forming lines and rapidly swimming laps across the pool. When they reached the other side, they formed a new line and swam back across. The lines moved fast, each swimmer following another in quick succession. Coach Bob watched the swimmers, helping them improve their speed.

"Laura, I think you might try to make your freestyle stroke a bit smoother," Coach Bob told a twelve-year-old girl in line in front of T.J. The coach moved his arms to show Laura what he meant. Then he moved on to another person.

"Hey, Laura," hissed Jake, who happened to be standing nearby. "Why don't you ask T.J. to help you? He's real good at giving swimming lessons, aren't you, T.J.?" Jake and his buddies laughed cruelly.

"Shut up, you nerds," Laura responded. She dove into the water and swam her lap across the pool. T.J. followed her and Zack followed T.J.

"How would you guys like to get back at Jake for all the mean things he's done?" Laura asked T.J. and Zack as soon as they had all reached the other side.

"Sure!" The boys did not hesitate.

"Do you see where Molly is standing by that tree?" Laura pointed directly across the pool. One of her friends was leaning over a big, circular pot that surrounded a tree. It looked like Molly was playing with the dirt in the pot.

"Yeah, what's Molly doing?" T.J. asked Laura.

"We're making a nice, muddy surprise for Jake," Laura grinned. "Every time we swim to that side of the pool, we fill our hands with water and dump it into the pot of dirt around that tree. Then, while we're standing in line, we stir up the dirt and water with a stick to make mud. As soon as we have enough mud, we're going to dump it into that athletic bag that's sitting beside the tree. Do you know whose athletic bag that is?" Laura asked, her eyes twinkling.

"Jake's!" the boys exclaimed.

"Shhhhh," Laura warned. "Not so loud!"

The boys looked around fearfully, but Jake had not heard them. He was busy joking with his buddies.

It was soon time for Laura, T.J., and Zack to swim back across the pool. When they reached the other side, they each took a big handful of water to the pot around the tree. T.J. eagerly took his turn stirring the mud. It would take several more handfuls of water to make enough mud to fill the inside of Jake's athletic bag.

The boys could now hardly wait to swim back and forth across the pool. Molly, Laura, T.J., and Zack carried as much water as they could to the pot of dirt. The word soon spread to the other swimmers in their line. Those swimmers told others until it seemed as if the entire team were in on the plan. No one told Jake and his friends.

It wasn't long before the swimmers had made enough mud. They had to hurry to get it into the athletic bag before Coach Bob decided to stop this activity and go on to another. Of course, the mud could not be put into the bag when Jake was near. They had to wait until Jake and his buddies were in the water.

Fortunately, that was not too hard. The twelve-year-old boys had arranged things so that they all swam their laps at the same time. As soon as they were in the water, Molly, Laura, T.J., and Zack would scoop big globs of mud into Jake's bag.

At the same time, the children had to keep an eye out for Coach Bob. They knew that the coach would not approve of their activity. The other swimmers on the team helped keep the coach busy at the right times. They would then shield the four children as they washed the mud off their hands in the pool.

Everything went perfectly. The athletic bag was

filled to the brim with mud. Zack held the sides together as T.J. zipped it shut. From the outside, no one would guess there was a sticky, gooey mess inside Jake's bag. T.J. and the others could hardly wait for the bully to pick up his bag and discover the surprise. Everyone giggled secretly.

"What's so funny?" Jake demanded as he glared at some of the team members who had pointed at him and giggled.

"Oh, nothing," the children quickly looked away. But all up and down the different lines, the swimmers tried to hide their giggles.

Jake looked around suspiciously but could find nothing wrong. He frowned and scowled at them all.

That morning it seemed as if swim practice would never end. Everyone wanted to see Jake discover his bag full of mud. They all groaned loudly when Coach Bob told them they must swim a few long-distance laps before practice ended.

Coach Bob looked oddly at his group of anxious swimmers. "What's the matter?" he asked them. "We never quit this early."

Finally, thirty minutes later, the coach signaled the end of practice. Everyone smiled at one another and hung around the pool area, secretly

waiting for Jake to discover his surprise.

It wasn't too long before the bully walked over to his bag. He reached down and grabbed the handle straps. With a jerky motion, Jake managed to lift the bag about two feet in the air, but it was so heavy with mud that he dropped it immediately. The bag hit the ground with a thud. On impact, the zipper threads burst open and something gooey and squishy oozed out of the bag and dripped down its sides.

"OOOOAAAAYUUCK!" Jake hollered at the top of his lungs. His friends came running. They all stared at the bag with shocked faces.

No one on the swimming team could keep a straight face. Every member, from the youngest to the oldest, roared with laughter. T.J. laughed so hard that he had to lie down on the concrete and hold his stomach. It was the piercing whistle and loud shouts of Coach Bob that finally brought order to the team.

"I want everyone to be quiet!" the coach shouted angrily. "This is disgusting," Coach Bob pointed at the mud-soaked athletic bag. "I am sick and tired of all the fighting on this team. I want it to stop!" The coach looked around at all of his swimmers.

"I want whoever filled Jake's bag with mud to confess. If you did it or had any part in it, I want you to step across this line." The coach pointed to a large crack in the concrete.

T.J. gulped and looked at Zack, Laura, and Molly. T.J. was sure to be the prime suspect. Everyone knew of his troubles with Jake, and no one better than Coach Bob. Maybe if he admitted the crime early, the coach would not be so hard on him.

Taking a deep breath, T.J. stepped over the line. He glanced at Coach Bob who nodded at him and did not look at all surprised. The coach, however, was in for a big surprise when not only

Zack, but also Laura and Molly followed T.J.'s example and crossed the line. He was in for an even bigger surprise when, one by one, all of the rest of the swim team members crossed the line to join T.J. and his friends.

T.J., himself, was surprised. He looked around at his teammates. It was absolutely incredible. The entire swim team had taken a stand with him against Jake and his friends!

"Well," Coach Bob said when he finally found his voice. "I guess I can't punish all of you. Instead, I will ask that you each bring a dollar to swim practice tomorrow. We will help Jake buy a new athletic bag. That's the only fair thing to do as I see it," said the coach. He looked down at T.J.

T.J. frowned. *The really fair thing would be for Jake to buy me new goggles,* he thought, but he did not say it out loud.

Coach Bob continued to look at T.J. Perhaps he was thinking the same thing. He turned to Jake and said, "You really brought this trouble on yourself, you know. If you had acted like a decent person toward others, instead of being mean and hateful, this never would have happened. I suggest that you change your ways, or you will spend your life being hated by others."

The coach dismissed practice. Everyone hurried to grab their towels and shoes. No one wanted to remain at the pool with Jake and the bag of mud.

As T.J. grabbed his towel, he noticed something rather unusual. Jake was not wearing his normal scowl. The bully was not jeering at the other swimmers or making rude noises. Instead, Jake appeared to be lost in thought.

Hmmmm, I wonder if Jake is sorry that he's been so bad to everyone, T.J. thought. *It must be awful to know that everyone on the swim team hates you.*

T.J. shrugged. He ran to join Zack, Charley, and Megan on their way up the steps that led to the snack bar area where Mother was waiting for them. As they walked, they talked and laughed with the other children on the team. T.J. smiled. At least he knew one thing. He was way ahead of Jake. Everyone on the swim team liked T.J.

6

SECRET DISGUISE

The next morning, T.J. and Zack were excited. Their mothers had finally given them permission to ride their bicycles to swim practice. It was not very far—about twenty minutes by bicycle—and they only had to cross one busy street with a traffic light. Besides, Zack's older brother, Jeremy, was going to ride with them.

Jeremy was fourteen years old and, according to Zack, too much into girls and music. Jeremy often rode his bike to swim team practice. So did most of the older swim team members. It was the grown-up thing to do.

T.J. and Zack felt particularly grown-up as they sat on their bicycles and looped their goggles and towels around their necks just like the older boys. T.J. waved good-bye to Mother and Charley as he and Zack pedaled off behind Jeremy. Charley looked very sad. T.J. felt sorry for his little brother. Mother had said that Charley was too young to go with them. Mother would bring Charley and Megan to practice later.

The early morning was beautiful—sunny but not too warm. T.J., Zack, and Jeremy had a great time racing full speed down the Juniper Street hill. As soon as they reached the bottom, Jeremy pulled a rubber ball out of his swimming bag. It was about the size of a baseball. Grinning mischievously, Jeremy tossed the ball to Zack who caught it with one hand. Zack tossed the ball to T.J. who threw it back to Zack, and soon they had a game of three-way catch under way. Of course, it was a little difficult playing catch while riding a bicycle, but T.J. managed all right. They continued tossing the ball to one another as they rode along, making their throws more and more challenging.

T.J. did not think about the danger of the game until he leaned too far to the right, trying to catch an extra wide pass from Zack, and lost his balance. T.J. and his bike crashed to the pavement! Jeremy stopped his bike immediately, but Zack, who was busily watching T.J., ran full speed into Jeremy. The two brothers also crashed to the ground!

"Help!"

"Watch where you're goin'!"
"Ouch!"
"You nerd!"
"I'm bleeding!"
The boys yelled and hollered at one another. T.J. slowly got to his feet and picked up his bike. The bike was unhurt, but T.J. had a nasty cut on his elbow. His right leg was also scratched and bleeding.
Zack and Jeremy struggled to pull their bicycles apart. The front wheel of Zack's bike had smashed into Jeremy's left pedal, hopelessly entangling it in the spokes of the wheel. They worked and worked on the two bikes, finally having to bend a spoke on Zack's front wheel to free them. Pulling Jeremy's pedal out of the wheel, they were able to bend the spoke back into position.
"Next time watch where you're going," Jeremy growled at Zack.
"Sorry!" Zack snapped back.
The boys got back on their bikes. T.J.'s elbow was still bleeding. They all had scrapes and scratches on their legs.
"Do you have my ball?" Jeremy asked T.J. as they got ready to move on again.
"No," T.J. replied. "I think it bounced over

there." He pointed to a large clump of bushes by the side of the road.

"Oh, great!" Jeremy frowned. He and the two younger boys left their bikes and crawled among the bushes looking for the lost ball. They could not find it and gave up after a while.

"You owe me a ball," Jeremy told his younger brother.

"Me?" Zack cried. "Why me?"

"Because you're the one who threw it so screwy that T.J. couldn't catch it, and now it's lost!" Jeremy said.

Zack did not reply. He just scowled at his older brother. T.J. rode behind them feeling very uncomfortable. He almost wished they had not decided to ride with Jeremy to the pool. He was sure his friend Zack was thinking the same thing.

The boys traveled on to the stoplight and crossed the one busy street between them and the pool. On the other side of the street was a bicycle path. It led all the way to the swimming pool.

As soon as they had crossed the street, Jeremy stopped his bike to talk with several older girls who were also on their way to swim practice.

"Go on ahead," Jeremy told Zack and T.J. "The pool's just straight ahead a few blocks. I'll catch up with you later."

"But, Jeremy," Zack objected, "Mom said we were supposed to stay with you the whole way."

"I'm only stopping for a few minutes," Jeremy sighed and winked at the girls. "You and T.J. go on ahead, and stop acting like a baby!"

"I'm not acting like a baby!" Zack shouted at his brother. He jerked his bike around and rode off at top speed. T.J. had to hurry to keep up with his friend.

"Hey, Zack, wait up!" T.J. hollered. He pulled alongside of Zack. "You can slow down now. Jeremy's way back there."

"He makes me so mad!" Zack cried. "He always thinks he's so cool!"

"Yeah," T.J. nodded his head. Maybe he was better off not having an older brother after all.

The boys rode in silence for another block. Zack finally slowed his pace. They were just beginning to enjoy the ride again when T.J. suddenly spotted trouble ahead.

"Quick! Stop your bike!" T.J. hissed loudly at Zack. The boys slid to a stop.

"What's the matter?" Zack asked anxiously.

"Jake!" T.J. answered and pointed to where Jake and his friends sat on their bicycles in the middle of the path, blocking the way for other bicyclists.

"Hurry! Hide behind those bushes," directed T. J. The boys quickly pulled their bicycles behind a row of bushes that lined the far side of the path.

"Now what do we do?" Zack asked as he and T.J. peered around the bushes at Jake and his friends.

"I dunno," T.J. looked worried. "I'd sure hate to meet up with Jake after what we did to his bag yesterday."

"That makes two of us," Zack agreed.

"I guess all we can do is to wait until Jake leaves and then follow him to the pool," decided T.J.

"But then we'll be late to practice," Zack replied. "You know how Jake is always getting there late."

"But what else can we do?" T.J. asked.

"Let's try and catch my brother when he comes by," suggested Zack. "Maybe he'll know what to do."

The boys waited and waited for Jeremy to show up. Just when they were ready to give up, Zack spotted his older brother moving slowly up the path. He was walking with a group of girls. They all pushed their bicycles. From the sound of it, they were having a lively conversation.

"That figures," Zack said disgustedly. "Jeremy's

always hanging around the girls."

T.J. frowned. That clinched it. He was doubly glad he didn't have an older brother!

Finally, Jeremy and his girlfriends reached a spot in the path directly across from the row of bushes.

"Psssst! Jeremy!" the younger boys hissed. But Jeremy and the girls were talking too loud and did not hear them.

"Jeremy!" Zack finally hollered. His older brother turned his head and stared at the row of bushes. He laughed when he caught sight of Zack and T.J. crouched behind the shrubs.

"Zack, what are you doing?" Jeremy called loudly.

"Shhhh! Come here," Zack waved Jeremy over to them.

Jeremy sighed and rolled his eyes upwards. "Excuse me," he told the girls, "I have to meet my brother in the bushes."

The girls giggled.

"Jeremy, this is serious," Zack said as soon as his brother joined them. "Jake and his buddies are blocking the path, and Jake hates T.J. and me, especially after we filled his bag with mud yesterday. If T.J. and I try to ride our bikes past them, we'll get murdered!"

"Hmmmm," Jeremy rubbed his chin. "I see what you mean."

"What should we do?" Zack asked his brother.

"Allison, come here," Jeremy called to one of the girls. "We need your help."

"Oh, great," Zack muttered.

Jeremy explained the situation to Allison and her friends. The girls thought for a minute. Then Allison snapped her fingers. "I've got it!" she said. "We'll disguise you!"

"Huh?" T.J. and Zack replied.

"Quick, take off your shirts and goggles!" Allison told the younger boys.

They did as they were told. Allison took each boy's shirt and wrapped it around his head in the form of an East Indian turban. Not one hair on the boys' heads remained visible. She then stretched the goggles around the turbans to hold them in place. Next she tied towels around the boys' necks to cover as much of their faces as possible.

"Perfect!" everyone agreed at once. Jake would not recognize them now.

All the same, T.J. felt nervous as he rode his bicycle straight toward the group of bullies. Jeremy rode in the lead, while Allison and her friends rode on either side of Zack and T.J.,

keeping them as concealed as possible.

"Hey, what's the hurry?" Jake called to Jeremy as soon as Zack's brother reached the bully.

"Aw, no hurry," Jeremy replied calmly. "Just moving on." He rode around the group. The others followed.

"Don't you want to stay here with us, Allison?" Jake teased as the girls rode past him. "Hey! Who are those weird-looking dudes?" Jake pointed at T.J. and Zack.

"Oh, just some friends of mine," Allison called back to the bully.

T.J. and Zack braced themselves as they rode

their bikes past Jake, practically under his nose. "Please, God, don't let him recognize us," T.J. silently prayed.

The big bully showed no sign of recognition. Indeed, when the boys looked back at him, Jake was gazing after them, scratching his head with a puzzled look on his face.

As soon as they had rounded a bend in the path, they all whooped with laughter. They had pulled one over on Jake Flaherty, and that was no easy thing to do.

T.J. looked at Allison. It was her idea that saved them. "Thanks for helping us," he told her shyly.

"Oh, sure, T.J.," Allison smiled. "I was happy to help you and Zack. Now if it had been Jeremy, that might have been a different story," she teased.

"Hey!" Jeremy protested and they all laughed.

Maybe big brothers aren't so bad after all, T.J. thought, *as long as they have girlfriends like Allison!*

7

TO THE RESCUE

T.J. and Zack reached the swimming pool with no further trouble. They even had a few minutes to spare, so they cleaned up their cuts from the bicycle accident.

Coach Bob put the team through a tough practice session that morning. A big swimming meet was coming up at the end of the week. Three other swim teams would be competing against them. The meet was to be held at their own swimming pool, Kingswood Country Club.

Everyone was tired at the end of practice. T.J. could hardly drag himself out of the pool. He begged Mother to let him, Zack, Charley, and Megan rest until the snack bar opened and then have an early lunch. Mother agreed. She let them relax around the pool area while she took Elizabeth to the rest room.

T.J., Zack, Charley, and Megan sat at the deep

end of the pool. They hung their feet over the edge and let them rest in the cool water.

The four children could hear the group of twelve-year-old boys as they made a commotion at the diving pool. The boys were performing as many strange and funny-looking dives with as much noise as they could. Coach Bob had asked them to stop, but they paid no attention to his order.

Suddenly, frantic shouting from the nearby diving pool alerted T.J. Something was wrong.

"HELP ME!" came a cry. T.J. and the others hurried over to the diving pool to see what was happening. There he saw Jake Flaherty thrashing wildly about in the water right beneath the high diving board. He was hollering for help. His buddies, instead of becoming alarmed, pointed at him and laughed.

"Cut it out, Jake, quit messing around!" called one of his friends.

"Jake, you faker, get out of the water!" hollered another.

"Help!" Jake continued to call, although his voice grew softer with every call.

T.J. stared at Jake. Was he pretending to drown, or was he really drowning? If Jake was pretending, he was certainly putting on a good show. T.J. watched as Jake suddenly doubled over in the water. His face contorted in pain. He gasped one more time and then sank under the water.

His twelve-year-old friends applauded wildly for their leader's performance. T.J., however, felt his heart leap in fear. He was sure that the look on Jake's face had been one of real terror. Somehow, T.J. knew that Jake was not faking. Jake was really drowning!

"Hurry! Go get Coach Bob!" T.J. told Zack, Charley, and Megan. "Tell him that Jake is drowning in the diving pool."

With frightened looks on their faces, the children rushed off to find the coach.

T.J. knew he couldn't wait for Coach Bob. Something had to be done now. He knew not to jump into the water after Jake—drowning victims usually grab their rescuers and pull them under the water, trying to save themselves. Instead, T.J. grabbed a long pole that hung down from a nearby lifeguard chair. He had seen lifeguards use it to help people out of the water. Carefully, T.J. lowered the pole into the water and extended it toward Jake.

The group of twelve-year-old boys stopped laughing. They stared in disbelief as T.J. tried his best to rescue their friend.

Jake had stopped thrashing and was making only feeble splashes. For an instant, T.J. was afraid that Jake would not have the energy to take hold of the pole. But almost the moment the pole touched Jake's arm, he grabbed it and pulled it with such a force that T.J. was knocked off balance. Standing at the edge of the pool, T.J. started to slip. He tried to catch himself but fell headfirst into the water.

When he pushed his head above water, T.J. saw that he was near Jake. The older boy still had hold of the pole, but now there was no one holding the other end. There was no one to pull him safely to the edge of the pool. Fear and panic were written all over Jake's face.

T.J. quickly grabbed onto the pole and tried to swim using one hand and his feet. He hoped he could pull Jake the short distance to the edge of the pool, but his plan did not work. T.J. found himself being pulled backward by the larger boy.

"HELP!" T.J. gasped, fighting with all of his strength to move forward. Soon, he would be within Jake's reach. He knew that the twelve year old would overpower him easily.

"HELP!" T.J. cried one last time as he felt Jake's arms seize him and pull him completely under the water.

Then, quite suddenly, another pair of arms grabbed T.J. and raised him above the water. Gasping for air, T.J. heard shouts all around him. Somebody had also taken hold of Jake. Strong arms pulled both of them backward to the side of the pool.

"Just relax and let us carry you," T.J. heard Coach Bob's voice just above his left ear. T.J. readily obeyed. He felt so tired after his struggle with Jake. He wondered if Jake was okay, but he did not have the strength to move his head to look. He floated along in the water and concentrated on taking deep breaths.

When they reached the side of the pool, Jake was lifted out to the concrete where Coach Bob immediately began rescue procedures. Several hands pulled T.J. from the water. T.J. was surprised to see that his rescuers were Jake's friends. They wrapped a towel around T.J.'s shoulders.

"T.J.!" his mother suddenly shouted. She ran up and hugged him. After making sure that T.J. was all right, Mother sat down beside him on the concrete. They watched Coach Bob's efforts to revive Jake.

As the coach worked on Jake, T.J. and Mother prayed, "Please, Lord Jesus, make Jake be all right. Please help him to breathe and make him as good as new. We pray in Your name. Amen."

A few seconds later, Jake began to come around. He coughed up water and began to breathe normally on his own. The paramedics arrived seconds later and took charge of things.

"T.J., you did a fine job," Coach Bob said, coming to stand by T.J. and his mother. "Using the pole kept Jake above water long enough to save his life."

"But I fell in the water," T.J. told his coach. "I wasn't able to pull Jake out."

"It doesn't matter," the coach assured him. "The important thing is that you tried your best to save Jake. I'm very proud of you."

"So am I," agreed Mother. She kissed T.J.

"Aw, Mom!" T.J. wiped his face, embarrassed that his mother had kissed him in front of the twelve-year-old boys.

"You saved our friend, T.J.," one of the older boys finally spoke up. "Thank you."

"You saved him and almost drowned yourself," added another. "You are an awesome dude!"

One by one, the older boys shook hands with T.J. Some patted him on the back. It was a wonderful moment—one T.J. would not forget for a long time.

"Thank You, Lord Jesus, for answering our prayer and making everything turn out so neat," T.J. silently prayed.

The paramedics put Jake on a stretcher and carried him to the ambulance. Even though he seemed normal, they were taking him to the hospital to make sure that he was all right.

Mother took T.J. and the other children home. After swallowing so much water, T.J. did not even want to be near a swimming pool that day. He watched television with Sergeant's big head resting on his lap. He also played quiet games with Charley, Megan, and Elizabeth.

When Father got home, he picked up T.J. and held him tight. T.J. did not mind. He didn't even mind when Father sat down in his favorite easy chair and sat T.J. on his lap.

"Your mother called me at the office and told me what a wonderful thing you did today," Father said to T.J. "I am very proud of you. This is for you." Father handed T.J. a big box.

Eagerly, T.J. opened the lid. He gasped in surprise.

"Well, what is it?" Mother, Charley, and the girls asked impatiently.

T.J. stared inside the box for another moment. Then he pulled out a shiny gold trophy. Its base was narrow, but it opened up at the top to form a heart shape. In the center of the heart was a round cup. Engraved on the cup were the words, "To my son, Timothy John Fairbanks, Jr., in memory of his daring rescue." The date was also engraved.

"Wow!" breathed T.J. when he read the inscription.

"This trophy is called a loving cup," said Father. "I thought you ought to have it because of the great love you showed today toward an enemy. Jesus said to love your enemies. Today you proved that your heart is big enough to do that. Today, you showed the world that you have a heart like Jesus."

8

THE GREATEST PRIZE

T.J., Charley, and Megan worked hard getting ready for the big swim meet to be held on the coming weekend. T.J. was both excited and nervous. He didn't want anything to stop him from winning his butterfly race this time.

Jake had not returned to practice after his near-drowning experience. T.J. wondered if perhaps Jake felt guilty because T.J. had tried to rescue him after Jake had been so mean, or maybe Jake felt bad because none of his friends had tried to help him. Whatever the reason was, the bully stayed away from them all.

Saturday finally arrived—the day of the big swim meet. The whole family was up early as the children had to be at the pool by eight o'clock. The meet did not start until nine, but Coach Bob wanted his swimmers warmed up and stretched out well before the races began.

"So this is the big day!" Father exclaimed as he sat down at the breakfast table.

"Yeah!" all three children answered.

"Yeth!" cried Elizabeth, a second later.

They all laughed.

"Let me tell you something," Father said. He reached over and put Megan on his knee. "I want each of you to do your best and, if possible, to win your races today. But I also want you to know that there's more to it than winning. It's more important to be a good competitor. You must be fair, be a good sport, and follow the rules. Not everybody can make it to the finish line first, but if you give it your best, you'll be a winner whether you place first, second, third, or even last." Father smiled at his children. "Why don't we pray for all of you to do well today?" he asked.

"Okay," the three children replied. They bowed their heads.

"Dear Father in heaven," Father prayed, "please help T.J., Charley, and Megan do their very best as they swim their races today. Help them to be good sports and to know that we love them whether they win or lose. We pray in Jesus' name. Amen."

When they arrived at the pool, Coach Bob started the children on their warm-up laps right away. He then led them in stretching exercises out of the pool so that the other teams had a chance to swim warm-up laps.

Everyone was excited. The swimming pool looked very festive. Rows and rows of deck chairs lined the pool area. Canopies were stretched overhead to keep the sun off the spectators. Big tents were pitched on the lawns surrounding the pool area for swimmers to rest in the shade between races.

T.J. paced around the pool area. He was a bit nervous. He knew it wouldn't be long before he would be up on the starting blocks.

The butterfly races were always the first to run. There were no butterfly races in Megan's age-group, so Charley was the first swimmer to represent the Fairbanks family. T.J. cheered his brother to the finish line. Even though the butterfly was not Charley's best stroke, he managed to pull in third out of eight swimmers. He would collect a white ribbon for that race.

After the girls' race, it was time for T.J.'s first race. While the timers got ready, T.J. jumped into the pool to get wet again. He wanted to be completely used to the water.

Climbing out of the pool and onto the starting block, T.J. heard several voices shouting his name.

"COME ON, T.J.!"
"YOU CAN DO IT, T.J.!"
"LET'S GO, T.J.!"

Embarrassed, T.J. looked around. Who was yelling his name so loudly? Finally, he spotted them. It was the group of twelve-year-old boys. They were gathered around Jake who sat on a deck chair at the side of the pool. Jake was dressed in street clothes, apparently not ready to swim in the meet.

"WIN THE RACE FOR ME, T.J.!" Jake hollered. He held his thumb in the air, giving T.J. the "go for victory" sign.

T.J. grinned back at Jake. It was amazing! Who would have ever thought that Jake would cheer for him? As T.J. bent into the diving position and waited for the starting gun to fire, he decided that he was going to win this race. He was going to win it for Jake!

The gun fired. T.J. was the first one off the blocks and into the water. He let himself glide just below the water's surface, carried by the force of his dive. When he broke above the surface of the water, he allowed himself a vigorous kick before moving his arms. In that way, T.J. covered half the width of the pool before taking a stroke. When he did break the surface with his arms, he

was more than a body length ahead of the other boys in the race.

Using the powerful butterfly double stroke and kick, T.J. propelled his way up and back the width of the pool. No one else had a chance. No one even came close. T.J. was the winner by a landslide!

When T.J. reached the finish, he stood up in the water and raised his arms high in victory. He knew he had just swum the best race of his life.

"Congratulations, T.J.!" Coach Bob shouted to T.J. "You just broke the district record for the nine-and-under boys' fifty-meter butterfly!"

An announcement over the public address system broadcast the news to the spectators.

When T.J. climbed out of the water, Jake was waiting for him behind the starting area.

"I guess I'll have to cheer for you more often," grinned Jake. "I had no idea you'd break a district record."

"I didn't either," T.J. laughed.

"Uh, T.J.," Jake said a little awkwardly, "thanks for coming to my rescue the other day. You saved my life. This is for you." Jake handed T.J. a small package.

T.J. opened it. Inside was a pair of brand-new goggles. "Gee, thanks," T.J. smiled. "I'll wear them when I swim my next race. Are you coming back to the team?" he asked Jake.

"Oh, yeah," Jake replied. "I'm just taking a little break. I'll be back, and from now on, we'll be friends!"

"That sounds good to me," smiled T.J.

The next few races went fast for T.J. He finished third in the backstroke (his worst stroke), but he got second in the breaststroke, just one second slower than the winner. Charley surprised everyone by coming in first in the seven-and-under boys' breaststroke. The two brothers enjoyed congratulating each other.

After lunch and a rest period, the team geared up for the freestyle races and relay races. Megan would swim in the first race of the afternoon—the five-and-under freestyle.

"Do you want me to take you over to the starting blocks?" T.J. asked Megan when the announcement was made for the start of her race.

"No, I can go by myself," Megan told him. She picked up her goggles and began to walk to the other side of the pool.

Mother and Father laughed at the frown on T.J.'s face.

"Don't worry, T.J.," Father said, "it's all part of being a coach. If she wins, then you'll get part of the credit."

"I just wish she wouldn't be so stubborn," T.J. told his parents. "I only wanted to remind her of a few things before the race."

T.J. watched anxiously as Megan positioned herself at the edge of the pool. Megan had done well the other night when she raced against swimmers from one other team, but today there were swimmers from three other teams to beat.

"Please God, help her do it again," T.J. prayed silently. He watched the other swimmers bend over, and the official raise his hand to fire the starting gun. BLAM!

T.J. and the family cheered loudly for Megan. She made a good dive. Now, if only . . . if only . . . YES! Megan came up quickly and pulled ahead in the race. T.J. hollered his head off as Megan fought neck and neck with a larger swimmer from another team, but in the end, his light-weight little sister triumphed, darting over the water like a bug!

The whole family shouted with glee. Megan had come in first again!

"Way to go, Megan!" T.J. pulled his sister from the water and clapped her on the back, nearly causing her to fall over. She didn't care. As soon as she caught her breath, Megan happily grinned from ear to ear. She ran back to where their parents were seated. They greeted her with open arms.

Not long after that, Charley's freestyle race began. T.J. shouted loudly as he watched his six-year-old brother beat all but one of the seven year olds. Charley won second place in the race.

T.J. managed to win his freestyle race, barely beating the second-place swimmer by half a second.

All in all, it was a fantastic swim meet for the Fairbanks family. The children happily showed one another their ribbons, no one more proud than Megan. Finally, as the family was preparing to leave, a group of swimmers from the team surrounded T.J., including Allison, the girl who had disguised T.J. and Zack and helped them escape Jake and his friends on the bicycle path.

"T.J., we have a very serious question to ask you," Allison said for the group.

"Huh?" T.J. was surprised. He wondered what all these people wanted with him. Was he in trouble or something?

Allison smiled. She pulled a little girl out from behind her back. So did the others. They all seemed to have small children with them.

"We were wondering, T.J., if you would like to coach our little brothers and sisters?" asked Allison.

Everyone laughed, including T.J. "No way," he said. "One is enough for me!"

T.J. was happy as he climbed into the family van for the ride home. He counted his ribbons—two blues, one red, and a white. He had done well at the swim meet. So had Charley and Megan. But there was more to being a winner than just winning races and collecting ribbons. T.J. knew that the greatest prize had been winning Jake's friendship. That was possible only because he had a certain kind of heart that was big enough to love an enemy. What had his father said? God had given T.J. a heart like Jesus, and that made him a special kind of winner.

T.J. gazed out the back window and up into the summer sky. "Thank You, Lord," he whispered.

Amen.

The Pet That Never Was

"What are you bringing to show and tell, T.J.?"

His mom is coming up the stairs, his best friend, Zack, is stuck in a tree just outside the window of his third-story bedroom, and the rest of the guys are waiting at the front door to see an eight-foot pet boa constrictor that T.J. doesn't have and never did.

How could one innocent question land T.J. in so much trouble?

The Fastest Car in the County

"I'll have the fastest and neatest looking car in the whole pack!"

T.J. wants his first Pinewood Derby car to be a winner. It looks like it will be, too. He and Father got the shape just right, evened out all the nicks and gauges, and sanded it super smooth. T.J. is certain his car is a winner, that is until his little sisters, Megan and Elizabeth, destroy it with pink crayon and stickers.

How can a pink car covered with stickers win the Pinewood Derby? T.J. wants to get even with them, but is that what God wants him to do?

Chariot Books™
David C. Cook Publishing Co.

Project Cockroach

"We'll go down in Jefferson School history."

That's what Ben Anderson promises when he gets Josh to agree to his plan. And turning loose a horde of cockroaches in Mrs. Bannister's desk drawer does sound impressive. Josh knows what Wendell, his peculiar next-door neighboor and classmate, would say, but what would you expect from a kid who actually goes to the library in the summertime?

Josh's mom wants him to be a good student and stay out of trouble. His long-distance dad back in Woodview wants him to "have a good year." Wendell wants him to go to church. But Josh isn't sure that even God can help him find answers to the questions in his life. He just wants to make a few friends and fit into his new world . . . even if it means taking a risk or two.

ELAINE K. McEWAN, an elementary school principal and the mother of two grown children, knows a lot of kids like Josh.

The Best Defense

"You sure know how to make a mother worry."

Josh has lived in Grandville barely two months, and he's already met the paramedics, the police, some teenaged would-be thugs, and a long-haired leather worker named Sonny. No wonder his mom gets a little anxious from time to time.

Josh thinks karate lessons would take care of some of his worries, but they aren't likely to help his relationship with Samantha Sullivan, the bossiest kid in the fifth grade. And they won't make his dad call more often.

Sonny tells him the key to conquering his fear is prayer . . . but Josh isn't sure that prayer is the answer. He needs to explore the possiblility. What if it doesn't work in a dark tunnel when he's facing two thugs?

ELAINE K. McEWAN, an elementary school principal and the mother of two grown children, knows a lot of kids like Josh.